rown

LITTLE TIGER PRESS
London

Mo was bored.

Bored, bored, bored.

"There must be
SOMETHING
amazing I can do,"
Mo said.

Ernestine was making
incredible ice creams.
"That's IT!" cried Mo.
"I can do that!"

"I'll be **MARVELLOUS** Mo — **King** of **sprinkles!**"

"Triple Whippy, coming up!"

sNAp!

Alphonse was brilliant with balloons.

"I can do **THAT.** They'll call me

MAGNIFICENT MO
POWer-puffer!"

"Oops!"

"oh NO, No, No!
Too MUCH Puff!"

At last Mo found the PERFECT thing.

"Now this looks totally fabulous!" he said.

"I'll be Mo the Majestic – HAIRDO HERO!"

"I'm not coming out again. EVER!"

"Don't give up, Mo," said his friends. "You'll find SOMETHING SPECIAL to do!" Just at that moment they heard a commotion . . .

"HELP! HELP!"

"What's the panic, Percival?" asked Mo.
"Big Ron has stolen the Golden Dodo!"
Percival squeaked. "We need YOU, Mo!"

"ME? Why me?"

"You're **super-strong!**
You're **super-fast!**"
cried Percival. "Only YOU
can catch Big Ron!"

"Fantastic!" said Mo. "At last!
Something amazing I can do!"

"Hey you, not so fast!"

"Come back, you big striped sardine!"

"This calls for something REALLY spectacular . . ."

"G

OTCHA!"

"Put me down!"
Big Ron yelled.

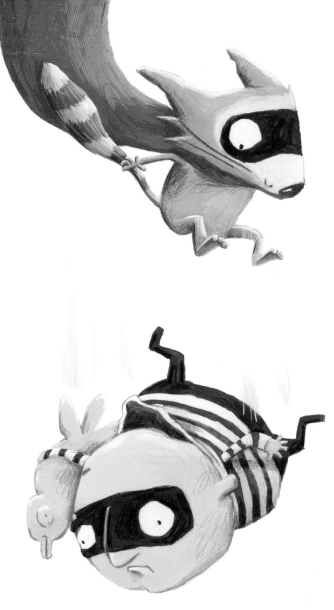

And so Mo did
just that . . .

. . . right into a **BIG** pile of elephant poo!

"**My** lovely robbery – **RUINED!**" Big Ron blubbed.

"You're nothing but a **rotten raccoon!**"

Mo smiled. "I'm not just ANY raccoon . . ." he said. "I'm Mo . . ."